D0944076

BILL BOWERBIRD
AND THE
>UNBEARABLE≋
BEAK-ACHE

Tyler Clark Burke

Owlkids Books

For my children, Rooksby & Hugo—TCB

Text & illustrations © 2017 Tyler Clark Burke

Owlkids Books acknowledges the financial support of the Canada Council for the Arts, the
Ontario Arts Council, the Government of Canada through the Canada Book Fund (CBF)
and the Government of Ontario through the Ontario Media Development Corporation's
Book Initiative for our publishing activities.

Published in Canada by
Owlkids Books Inc.
10 Lower Spadina Avenue
Toronto, ON M5V 2Z2

Published in the United States by
Owlkids Books Inc.
1700 Fourth Street
Berkeley, CA 94710

Library and Archives Canada Cataloguing in Publication

Burke, Tyler Clark, author

     Bill Bowerbird and the unbearable beak-ache / Tyler Clark Burke.

ISBN 978-1-77147-154-1 (hardback)

     I. Title.

PS8603.U73765B55 2017   jC813'.6   C2016-903292-2

Library of Congress Control Number: 2016910567

Edited by: John Crossingham
Designed by: Alisa Baldwin

ONTARIO ARTS COUNCIL
CONSEIL DES ARTS DE L'ONTARIO
an Ontario government agency
un organisme du gouvernement de l'Ontario

Canada Council
for the Arts

Conseil des Arts
du Canada

Canadä

Manufactured in Dongguan, China, in November 2016, by Toppan Leefung Packaging & Printing (Dongguan) Co., Ltd.
Job #BAYDC32

A   B   C   D   E   F

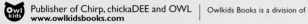 Publisher of Chirp, chickaDEE and OWL | Owlkids Books is a division of Bayard CANADA
www.owlkidsbooks.com

Bill Bowerbird is a
very special bird.

He has a felt cap and blue boots,
a rooster's comb, a copper flute,
a lion's pride for loot and trash,
a broken bike, a runway sash.

But Bill has one thing he'd like to shake—
He's got a terrible,
UNBEARABLE,
lousy beak-ache!

"What to do, what to do?"
Bill loudly wails.
"Please help me, friends,
to cure this ail!"

His knickers a-knot,
his feathers askew,
*"Wickety-tickety
BOO-hoo-hoo!"*

So down to the owl near the foot of the tree.

"Try this—*hoot, hoot*—the honey's on me!"

That didn't work—
guess it's time for a walk.
Maybe the zebras
could give him a talk?

"We don't really have
any words of advice.
Do you think it would help
if you borrowed our stripes?"

"I'll carry these home
to see if they work.
But first I should check
with the town-hall clerk."

The walrus is in and she sure looks smart,
dapper and dancing—what a good start!

Maybe *she* has a trick
to make a sore beak nice?
"How 'bout this carrot?
It's frozen like ice!"

But nothing felt better!
Bill's head was afire—
Isn't there someone
out there he could hire?

He moped down the path
on the way to his house.
He queried a frog, a yak,
and a grouse.

Not one thing was helping,
his ache only grew—
*"Wickety-tickety
BOO-hoo-hoo!"*

And just when he'd almost given up hope,
he spotted two beavers doing tricks with a rope.

Bill joined the game, and between jumps asked,
"When—you—have—some—time—I—need—help—with—a—task."

"My head is aching,
not to mention this maw—
I really could use
some help with my jaw!"

"Here's a tree," said the beavers,
"all covered in bumps.
 Chew down these knobs
 'til you're just left with stumps."

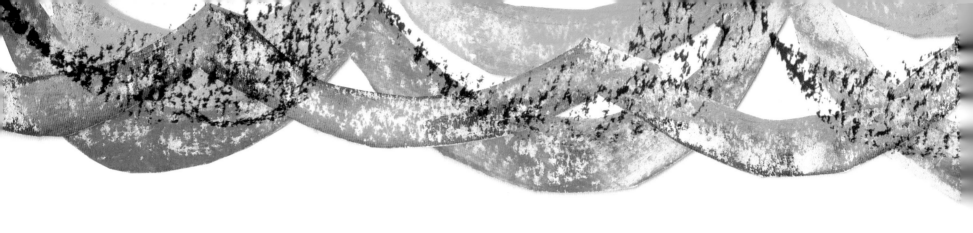

So Bill stumbled home and laid out his stuff…

...then SUDDENLY realized he wasn't feeling so rough!

He opened his beak,
and looked right inside…
Turns out a tooth
had come along for a ride!

Bill called outside
to tell all his friends.
They partied away
until that day's end.

Happy and tired, Bill emptied his nest.
It was time for everyone to get a good rest.

"A goodnight to me,
  A goodnight to you...
  Wickety-tickety
  WOO-hoo-hoo!"